DATE DUE

Put Beginning Readers on the Right Track with
ALL ABOARD READING™

The All Aboard Reading series is especially for beginning readers. Written by noted authors and illustrated in full color, these are books that children really and truly *want* to read—books to excite their imagination, tickle their funny bone, expand their interests, and support their feelings. With four different reading levels, All Aboard Reading lets you choose which books are most appropriate for your children and their growing abilities.

Picture Readers—for Ages 3 to 6
Picture Readers have super-simple texts, with many nouns appearing as rebus pictures. At the end of each book are 24 flash cards—on one side is the rebus picture; on the other side is the written-out word.

Level 1—for Preschool through First-Grade Children
Level 1 books have very few lines per page, very large type, easy words, lots of repetition, and pictures with visual "cues" to help children figure out the words on the page.

Level 2—for First-Grade to Third-Grade Children
Level 2 books are printed in slightly smaller type than Level 1 books. The stories are more complex, but there is still lots of repetition in the text, and many pictures. The sentences are quite simple and are broken up into short lines to make reading easier.

Level 3—for Second-Grade through Third-Grade Children
Level 3 books have considerably longer texts, harder words, and more complicated sentences.

All Aboard for happy reading!

To my two favorite monkeys,
Joe and Tommy—D.R.

Text and illustrations copyright © 2000 by Dana Regan. All rights reserved. Published by
Grosset & Dunlap, a division of Penguin Putnam Books for Young Readers, New York. ALL
ABOARD READING is a trademark of The Putnam & Grosset Group. GROSSET & DUNLAP
is a trademark of Grosset & Dunlap, Inc. Published simultaneously in Canada. Printed in the
U.S.A.

Library of Congress Cataloging-in-Publication Data is available.

ISBN 0-448-42414-2 (GB)   A B C D E F G H I J
ISBN 0-448-42299-9 (pb)   A B C D E F G H I J

ALL
ABOARD
READING™
Level 1
Preschool-Grade 1

Monkey See, Monkey Do

By Dana Regan

Grosset & Dunlap • New York

Monkey see,
monkey do.
Can you do
what they do, too?

Monkeys ride
and monkeys skate.
This one does
a figure eight.

Monkeys creep
and monkeys crawl.
I hope that this one
does not fall!

10

Monkeys jump
and monkeys shout.
Monkeys shake
their arms about.

Monkeys laugh...

...and monkeys cry.

Monkeys smile
and wave bye-bye.

16

Monkeys run
and monkeys hide.

Look for monkeys
far and wide.

Monkeys kiss
and monkeys hug.

Monkeys do
the jitterbug.

Hop on one foot, hop on two.
You can do what monkeys do!

Can you guess what monkeys eat?

They eat bananas
with their feet.

Monkeys yawn.

Do not make a peep.

Shhh…I think
the monkeys are asleep.
Good night.